Originally published as *Graag gedaan* in Belgium and the Netherlands
by Clavis Uitgeverij, 2019
English translation from the Dutch by Clavis Publishing Inc., New York

Visit us on the Web at www.clavis-publishing.com.

Little Book of Kindness written and illustrated by Francesca Pirrone

ISBN 978-1-60537-533-5

This book was printed in February 2020 at Grafiche AZ srl,
Viale del Lavoro 8, I-37036 San Martino Buon Albergo - Verona - Italy.

First Edition
10 9 8 7 6 5 4 3 2 1

Francesca Pirrone

Clavis
NEW YORK

It's easy to be kind . . .

Say thank you.

Offer a smile.

Be patient.

Lend a helping hand.

Nurture.

Protect.

Rescue.

Offer help.

Take turns.

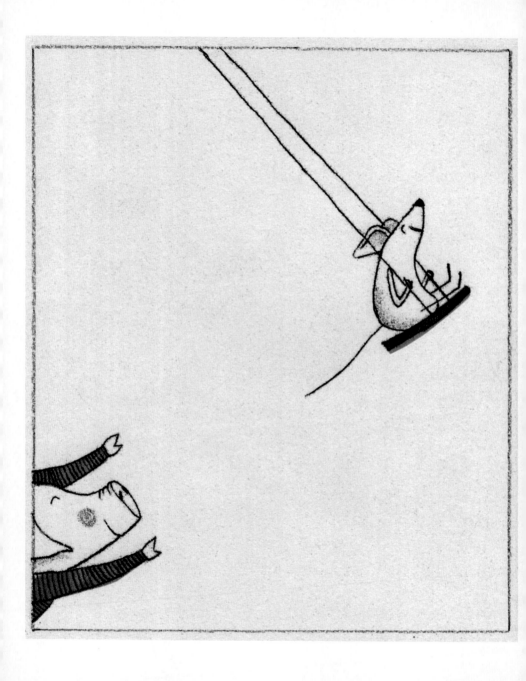

Share.

Respect the planet.

When you are kind,

others are kind too.